The Ghost in the Bath

by

JEREMY STRONG

Illustrated by Scoular Anderson

This is for ghost-hunters everywhere.
Make sure you always have a bucket of
water handy.

First published in 2012 in Great Britain by
Barrington Stoke Ltd
18 Walker St, Edinburgh, EH3 7LP

www.barringtonstoke.co.uk

ISBN: 978-1-84299-997-4

Printed in China by Leo

Contents

Chapter 1

Mrs Trouble and the Victorians

Luke had a problem. He wasn't sure if the problem was his new school, his new house, or Mrs Rubble. Maybe everything was a problem, thought Luke. Sometimes that was how it seemed to be.

School was OK, or at least it would be OK if it wasn't for Mrs Rubble. Mrs Rubble was Luke's teacher and the subject she liked best was History. Luke didn't like most subjects at all, including History. His only good subject at school was Home Time. And, oh yes, he liked Break Time as well and Lunch Time. They were good. But the bits in between were not so great.

"History is stupid," said Luke, wrinkling his freckled nose. "It's all about dead people."

"Yeah," said his new friend, Mohammed. "Dead people are – well, like, dead, aren't they?"

"And Maths is stupid too," Luke went on. "I mean, what's the point? I've got a calculator."

"Yeah," nodded Mohammed. "Maths is like, well." Mohammed stopped. What was Maths like?

"It's all numbers," Luke said. "Counting. And writing is stupid too, isn't it? Scribble, scribble, scribble. What's that all about? I

mean, why spend hours writing stuff down when you can just *tell* people it all?"

"Yeah, or you could text them," said Mohammed.

"That's almost the same as writing it down," Luke pointed out.

Mohammed was silent. In fact he quite liked writing, and Maths. But he liked Luke even more. Luke had straight, brown hair and Mohammed's was black and curly. He'd always wanted straight hair. On the other hand, Luke was shorter than he was. In fact everyone in class was shorter than Mohammed.

"What do you think of Mrs Rubble?" Luke asked.

"Don't know," Mohammed said. "What do you think of her?"

"I think," he said slowly, "Mrs Rubble is trouble."

Mohammed laughed. "Yeah. She's Mrs Trouble! So what are you going to do for the History project?"

Mrs Rubble wanted everyone to do a project about the Victorians. It could be anything to do with that time in history. The class had been full of ideas the day she told them about it.

"I'm going to do Jack the Ripper!" Jack shouted. "It's going to be full of blood! I'll call it 'Jack the Dripper', because he drips blood everywhere."

Grace shivered. "I'm going to do Florence Nightingale," she said. "She was a nurse who made people better."

"Jack the Dripper is better," said Jack. "He was a killer who made people worse!" Jack gave an evil laugh and stared hard at everyone. Jack had fierce blue eyes that seemed to look right inside you.

"You're horrid," said Grace.

"You're stupid," Jack said back, rubbing his short blonde hair. Jack liked Grace. She looked after the class goldfish. She was quiet and clever and pretty. She had a turned-up nose and green eyes. Grace wasn't stupid at all. In fact Jack felt stupid for saying she was stupid.

"That's quite enough," said Mrs Rubble before they could say any more. "I want your projects in by the end of the week. Luke, what will yours be about?"

Luke's mind went blank. It always went blank when Mrs Rubble spoke to him. Luke thought it must be the sound of her voice. It seemed to drive away any brain power he might have had. If only she'd keep quiet. He started to shrug his shoulders but then had the best idea ever. His eyes lit up.

"I'm going to do the Vikings!" he said.

Mrs Rubble sighed. "No you're not," she snapped. "The Vikings lived in Viking times. Do you know who lived in Victorian times, Luke? I will tell you. The Victorians. Go home, find out about them and write about them."

Now Luke sat at home and stared out of the window. The Victorians. What were they like? Boring, probably. He would have liked to ask one of them, but of course they were all dead. History. The only thing that seemed to happen in history was that everyone died.

Sometimes Luke thought it would be OK to be dead. At least then he wouldn't have to do stupid projects for Mrs Rubble. Mrs Trouble.

Chapter 2
A Surprise Visitor

When Luke got home he told his parents about the History project. He asked them what he could write about.

"Jack the Ripper," said Dad.

Mum shook her head. "Too much blood," she said. "What about Florence Nightingale?"

"You can't ask Luke to write about Floppy Night-gown!" said Dad. "That's girl stuff."

Luke sighed. Too much blood. Too much girly stuff. What could he write about? He thought about it all evening, until his brain felt like a bowl of cold porridge.

"It's almost time for bed," said Mum. "Go and have a bath. Maybe you'll get an idea while you're in there."

"More likely he'll get wet," said Dad, and laughed at his own joke.

Luke liked the bathroom in their new house. In fact, it wasn't really a new house at all. It was just new to them. The house itself was about 200 years old. The bathroom looked old too. The tub sat on four brass feet shaped like lion paws. The sides were high and you had to lift your legs up a lot to climb in.

Luke put the taps on, took off his clothes and climbed in. He put in a bit of bath foam and stirred up some big, fat bubbles. Then he lay back and closed his eyes. Lovely. His mind began to float away in a dream about a girl. She was standing beside him. She was tall and pretty and looked at least 18. She asked Luke what he was doing in Charlie's bath.

"I'm not in Charlie's bath," Luke told her. "This is my bath."

The girl got cross and stamped her foot. "No it isn't," she said. "It's Charlie's bath. Get out at once. You're not allowed to be in Charlie's bath."

"I keep telling you, this is not Charlie's bath. It's mine," insisted Luke.

The girl bent down and reached out to Luke with both hands. He thought she was going to choke him. This wasn't a dream – it was a nightmare! Luke decided to wake up. He opened his eyes.

"Argh!" yelled Luke. There WAS a girl in his bath! A GIRL was standing IN LUKE'S BATH!!

Luke hid as much of himself under the bubbles as he could. "What are you DOING?" he asked in shock. "How did you get in here? Why are you so … thin?"

The girl stood there with her hands on her hips. "I might ask you the same question. What are YOU doing here? This is my Charlie's house and my Charlie's bath, and you're in it and you shouldn't be. Get out!"

"I can't get out," said Luke. "Not while you're looking!"

"I won't look," said the girl. "I'll go away, count to ten and then come back." She stepped out of the bath and *PING!* she vanished.

Luke hopped out of the tub, grabbed the biggest towel he could find and folded it round his body. His mind was turning cartwheels. That girl had just vanished, right in front of his eyes. How did she do that?

PING! She was back, standing in the bath again.

"You're a ghost!" Luke said in a croak.

"Exactly," the girl said. "But you can only see me if part of my body is touching water."

Luke looked at her hard while he thought about this. "Right," he said. "So when you vanished just now, you didn't go anywhere, you were still here in the bathroom."

The girl nodded.

"You were still in the room when I got out of the bath and looked for a towel?" Luke said.

The girl nodded again. Luke turned very, VERY red.

"It doesn't matter," said the girl. "I'm a ghost. My name's Ellie, and Charlie and I were going to get married but I drowned."

Luke looked at the bath. "You drowned in Charlie's bath?" he asked.

"Of course not, stupid," snapped Ellie. "How old are you?"

"Eleven," Luke snapped back.

"Well, I think you're very silly for an eleven-year-old," Ellie said. Luke began to wonder if Mrs Rubble and Ellie were related in any way.

"Of course I didn't drown in his bath," Ellie said. "I drowned at sea. That's why you can only see me when part of me is in the water. I was on the *Titanic* when it sank."

Luke's eyes almost popped out of his head. "Wow!" he said. "The *Titanic*? You were really on the *Titanic*?"

Ellie nodded.

"And you really drowned? I mean, you're really, really dead?"

"Yes!" sighed Ellie, and then her face went all sad. "Charlie was on the *Titanic* too. We jumped into the water together. We were all right for a while, but the water was so cold. We couldn't hold on to each other any more. Our whole bodies had gone numb. We slipped away from each other. Everything was dark and cold. I drowned. Charlie must have drowned too."

Luke bit his lip. He didn't know what to say. It was too sad for him to say anything.

"I've been looking for Charlie ever since," said Ellie. "I've looked everywhere. I thought

15

that maybe if I came back to Charlie's house I might find him again. But then you were in his bath. I've got to find Charlie. I won't be at peace until I find him. We were meant to be together forever."

Luke swallowed. What a tragic story. He looked at Ellie. She seemed so lost and sad. Then all at once Luke sat bolt upright. He had just had the best idea ever.

"I know what to do," he told Ellie. "I am going to help you find Charlie. And in return, you can help me with my History project. I have got to do it about the Victorians. Now I know what to write about – the *Titanic*!"

"But the *Titanic* wasn't Victorian," Ellie pointed out. "Queen Victoria died a few years before it sank."

Luke waved a hand at her. "A few years one way or another won't matter," he said.

My teacher won't notice. Victorians, Vikings – it's all much the same thing."

"Vikings?" said Ellie, who had no idea what her new friend was going on about.

History was NOT Luke's best subject.

Chapter 3
Fight!

"Have you seen the ghost in the bathroom?" Luke asked Mum at breakfast.

"No," she said. "Is it a nice ghost or a creepy one?"

Luke could tell that his mum didn't believe him. But he needed to talk about Ellie and see what he could find out about her and Charlie.

"The ghost is OK," said Luke. "But I'm never sure when she's there." He blushed as he remembered what had happened the night before. "Do you know who used to live in this house, Mum?"

His mum shook her head.

"How long ago did the *Titanic* sink?" Luke asked.

"1912," said Dad, as he passed on his way to the kitchen. "Why do you want to know?"

"Just wanted to know," Luke said. "How could you find out who lived here before us, Mum?"

His mum shook her head again. "You've got a lot of questions this morning, Luke. I don't know. Maybe you can find out at the library. Is it part of your homework?"

Luke grinned. "Yes! And thanks!"

The library – of course. Why hadn't he thought of that? He'd drop in on his way from school.

When Luke got to class he told Mohammed about the ghost in the bathroom.

"A real ghost?" said Mohammed, his eyes getting bigger and bigger.

Luke nodded. "And she saw you in the bath?" Mohammed asked. His eyes almost popped out of his head. Luke nodded again.

"What did you do?" Mohammed asked.

"I said: *Hello, who are you?*" Luke said. "I was pretty cool in fact."

Luke knew that this was not what had happened, but he thought it was close enough. "The ghost is going to help me with my homework," he said.

"Wow!" breathed Mohammed. "I wish I could see a ghost."

"I'll bring her to school," said Luke. The words were out of his mouth before he knew it.

"Oh, wow," Mohammed said again. Before Luke could say any more Mohammed was telling the rest of class that Luke was going to bring a ghost into school. Grace was so shocked she almost tipped a whole tub of fish food into the goldfish bowl. But Jack just sneered.

"I don't believe in ghosts." Jack said. He went cross-eyed, pulled a silly face and started to run all round the playground going "Wooooooo!" When he got back to the others he said that Luke hadn't seen a ghost at all.

"Yes I did," said Luke.

"No you didn't," said Jack. "I bet it was just your own foot sticking up out of the water."

"You're stupid," shouted Luke, and they began pushing and shoving each other. Luke tripped over his own feet and fell to the ground. Jack jumped on top.

"Fight! Fight!" shouted the class.

The next minute Mrs Rubble had appeared in the playground. She pulled Luke and Jack to their feet and demanded to know what the fuss was about. Mohammed was very happy to tell her.

"Whose fault was it?" asked Mrs Rubble.

"His," said Luke and pointed at Jack.

"His," said Jack, and pointed at Luke.

"In that case you will both have to say 'sorry' to each other," said Mrs Rubble "Then Luke can stand at that end of the playground and Jack can stand at this end, and there will be no more play for either of you."

Luke stomped off to the far end of the playground. *Jack is an idiot,* he thought. *I'll get Ellie to come into school. That will show him! He'll be sorry then. And he'll feel a right loser too. Good!*

Chapter 4
A Visit to the Library

On his way home from school Luke popped into the library. He had never been in a library before. He had never seen so many books before, either. Luke began to think that you could probably find out about anything in the whole world here.

He went to the main desk. Two women were there. One was young and she had a tight, thin mouth. When she spoke it looked as if she was trying to snap up flies and swallow them.

The other lady was much older, about the same age as Mrs Rubble, but with twinkly eyes and a smiley face. She winked at Luke. Luke wasn't used to old ladies winking at him. Most of the time they just glared.

"Can I help you?" asked the older lady.

"Children's books are over there," said the younger one, like she wanted rid of Luke.

"Can I help you?" asked the older lady again.

"I don't want a children's book," Luke whispered. "I want to know who lived in my house in the past."

"We're not detectives," snapped the younger woman, but the older lady waved at

Luke to follow her, and he did. They went all the way to the far back of the building.

"My name is Betty," the lady told Luke as they walked. "We keep records about people from this area on the computer. The records used to be in great big books but now it's all on computer so it's much easier to look things up. What's the name of the road you live in?"

Betty put the name of Luke's road and the number of his house into the computer. "Oh," she said as she read the screen. "Your house is quite old, isn't it?"

"Dad says it's 200 years old," said Luke.

"That means quite a lot of people have lived there," Betty said. "Was there any special date you had in mind?"

Luke shut his eyes tight. When did the *Titanic* sink? Dad had told him. He just had to get his brain to think!

"1912!" he shouted with a grin.

Betty scanned the screen, looking for dates. "Here we are," she said. "Edward Smith and his wife Flora lived there then."

Luke sighed. There was no record of Charlie. Betty saw the look on his face and asked if there was someone special he was searching for.

"It says here that they had five children," she read from the screen. "Daisy, Elsie, Peter, Charles and Susan."

"Charles! Charlie!" said Luke with a grin. "His name was Charlie Smith."

"There," smiled Betty. "You've found him."

"I want to know what happened to him," said Luke.

"Right," said Betty. "We need to look at another set of records for that. Hang on a minute while I get it up on screen. These are the records of births and deaths. Type his name in here."

Luke typed in CHARLES SMITH. Oh dear – there were records for twenty-three Charles Smiths.

"That's the trouble with popular names," said Betty. "Never mind, the records will show his address. Can you see the address of the house?"

"There!" Luke said, and jabbed a finger at the screen. "Charles Smith. Wounded in France, died March 15th, 1915" He looked at it again. "1915," he said again, in a soft voice.

"That was the middle of the First World War," said Betty. "He was wounded in France, fighting, and died when he got home."

"So he didn't drown," Luke said.

"Oh no," said Betty. "I expect he got shot, or blown up, or gassed. It was a terrible war. Is it important?"

Luke looked up at her and shook his head. "I don't know," he said. He had no idea if it was. "Only Ellie can answer that question."

"Who's Ellie?" asked Betty and she winked again. "Is she your girlfriend?"

Luke almost choked. He coughed, spluttered, turned a very deep red and got off his chair. "No," he said in as firm a voice as he could. "She's just – she's just someone who hangs around a lot where she's not wanted."

"Oh," said Betty.

"And she's wet," Luke added.

Chapter 5
More of Ellie

When Luke got home he went straight to the bathroom and locked himself in.

"Ellie?" he called. "Are you there?"

Then he waited. For a while he couldn't see or hear anything. At last a faint shape began to appear. It was Ellie, or at least it was some of Ellie. All Luke could see was one half of her body, and half her head. And she was standing in the toilet bowl.

"Yuck! Do you have to stand there?" asked Luke.

"Yes, because I have to be in contact with water, remember?" said Ellie.

"But I can only see half of you," Luke complained.

"I need lots of water to make a full appearance," Ellie told him. "That's why I stood in the bath last time."

"You're weird," Luke said.

"I'm a ghost," Ellie answered. "I'm meant to be weird."

"Yes, but you're even weirder," said Luke. "Ghosts don't appear in toilet bowls."

"Oh, you're an expert on ghosts now, are you?" Ellie asked. Then her lip started to wobble. "Do you think I want to be like this?"

she said. "Well, I don't. I didn't want to drown and I never wanted to be a ghost. It's not much fun."

Luke was shocked. He thought it would be ace to be a ghost. You would be able to slide through walls and appear in places whenever you wanted. You could scare people. Cool! But then he remembered that he had something to tell Ellie. "I've discovered more about Charlie," he said. "He didn't drown."

Ellie's hand flew to her mouth. "He didn't?" she asked. "Do you know what happened to him?"

"Two years after you drowned there was a war," Luke said. "Charlie was killed in the war, after fighting in France."

"Oh, poor Charlie," Ellie said softly. "Poor Charlie."

"It was only three years after the *Titanic* sank," Luke told her. "I also checked that Charlie wasn't married when he died."

Ellie gave a small smile and then asked Luke if he knew where Charlie was buried. Luke shook his head. "The library didn't have that information. Betty, the woman in the library, said I would need to check in church records to see where he was buried. I'll start on that tomorrow. I have to get on with my homework now. I told someone at school about you. They don't believe you're a ghost."

"I bet it was a boy who said that," said Ellie in a smug voice.

"You're right," Luke said. "It was Jack. How did you know it was a boy?"

"Boys are like that," Ellie said.

"Like what?" asked Luke.

"Stupid," said Ellie.

"Oh right," snapped Luke. "Boys are so stupid they can't even go to a library and find out all the things a stupid ghost can't find out for herself because she's too busy standing in a toilet bowl."

Luke was very surprised when Ellie burst out laughing at that.

"Now what?" he asked.

"You're funny," she told him. "All right. You've got a good point. Thank you for going and finding out all those things."

Luke was silent for a few moments.

"Have you forgiven me yet?" Ellie asked in her sweetest voice.

"Maybe," Luke said. "Anyway, I told the boys that you'd come into school with me tomorrow. They'll have to believe in you then. I'll take a big bucket of water with me and you can stand in it. It'll be so cool! I can't wait to see the look on Jack's face!"

"I'm not going," said Ellie.

"What!" Luke's grin vanished. "But you've got to!" he said.

Ellie shook her head. "I haven't got to at all, and I won't. I'm not going to your silly school, so there."

"But you've got to!" said Luke again.

"No I haven't. I'm not some kind of zoo animal you can put on show," Ellie told him.

"Well don't expect me to find Charlie then!" shouted Luke. He was so angry. Ellie was such a pain in the neck. He stared at her, standing there in the toilet, and his eyes blazed. Huh! He'd teach her a lesson.

He reached forward and pulled the chain. Then he stormed out, slamming the door as the toilet flushed behind him.

Chapter 6

More Trouble from Mrs Rubble

The next day, at school, Mrs Rubble asked how their projects were coming on. "Mohammed," she asked, "how about you?"

"I've finished," Mohammed said, and he beamed at everyone.

"How about you, Grace?" asked Mrs Rubble.

"I've done six pages," said Grace. "And I've found some photographs of Florence Nightingale."

"How thrilling," Jack said under his breath, only quite loud. Everyone heard him except Mrs Rubble, and the boys laughed.

"Jack?" said Mrs Rubble, fixing Jack with her steely eyes.

"I've done three pictures of Jack the Ripper murdering people and you can see blood spurting out of their necks," said Jack. "They're so cool!"

Mrs Rubble's eyebrows shot up her head. "I see, Jack. That sounds lovely. Perhaps you could do some writing too, without the blood. Now then, Luke, what have you been up to?"

"I'm collecting information," Luke said in a serious voice. He hoped that would be enough for Mrs Rubble. It wasn't.

"And what have you found out?" she asked.

"Um ..." began Luke. "I know who used to live in my house 100 years ago."

"Really? That sounds interesting. Do you know their name?"

"Charlie Smith," Luke said. "He was going to marry a girl called Ellie."

"Yeah, but Ellie drowned and she's a ghost," said Mohammed, his eyes big and round. The rest of the class laughed.

"Yeah, and Luke said he'd bring the ghost to school today," shouted Jack. "Only she's not here, because there's no such thing as ghosts. Luke's just a baby who believes in ghosts. Woooooo! He's making it all up."

"I am not!" shouted Luke, his face all red.

"Wooooo!" mocked Jack.

"That's enough!" shouted Mrs Rubble. "Now, I have no need to remind you that it's the end of the week tomorrow and your projects have to be in. I expect to see your work on my desk first thing in the morning. And Grace, do you think you could stop feeding that goldfish before it explodes?"

Luke was in a bad mood all day. The class thought he'd made it up, and he hadn't. It wasn't fair. It was all Ellie's fault. She was such a pain.

As the day went on Luke found himself thinking about Ellie more and more. What was it like to drown? Horrible. Bet it was scary too. And she lost Charlie, and he lost her. Poor Charlie. He survived the sinking of the *Titanic* only so he could be killed in a war. Now Ellie was stuck in Charlie's old house trying to find him so she could be at peace. And Luke was the only person who could help her.

After school Luke decided to take the long way back home. It would take him past three different churches. The first church was locked up and there was nobody around. The second church was open and Luke went in.

It was dark and cold and smelled a bit. A woman came out of the gloom.

"I'm the vicar," the woman told Luke. "Can I help?" Luke told her he needed to find out who was buried in the area.

"I'm afraid I can't tell you that," said the vicar. "Only adults can look at the records."

Luke nodded. "I'll just have to wait ten years then," he said. The vicar gave him a blank look. "That was a joke," Luke told her.

"Really?" said the vicar and she vanished into the gloom.

Much the same thing happened at the third church. After that, Luke went home, fed up with everything. He hadn't done his project. He had nothing written down and nothing to show Mrs Rubble. He hadn't found out where Charlie was buried either. He was useless.

Up in the bathroom he ran a bath for Ellie and soon she appeared. He could see all of her this time.

"What did you find out?" she asked, a keen look on her face.

Luke shook his head.

"Nothing." He told her about the church visits.

"At least you tried," Ellie said. "Thank you."

"Yeah, and now everybody at school thinks I'm stupid and I'm a liar because you didn't come to school with me today," Luke said. "Jack says ghosts don't exist. And I haven't done my project either."

Ellie frowned. "What if we give them all a shock then?" she asked. "What if I come to school with you tomorrow?"

"Really?" asked Luke, feeling better at once. "Would you do that?"

Ellie smiled. "I don't really want to, but you've tried to help me and maybe it would be fun to do something silly," she said.

Luke was ready to burst. "It'll be ace!" he said. "You wait and see. I'll find the biggest bucket ever and you can stand in that. Tomorrow is going to be so cool!"

Chapter 7
Buckets Galore!

At breakfast the next day Luke told his parents that he had to take a bucket into school. "Whatever for?" asked his dad.

Luke knew he couldn't tell his mum and dad the real reason, so what *could* he say? He couldn't think of anything.

"Mrs Rubble said," was the best he could come up with, after several moments hard thinking.

"All of you?" asked Mum. "Mrs Rubble wants twenty-seven buckets?"

"Yes," lied Luke. He had his fingers crossed under the table so the lie didn't count.

Mum looked at Dad. Dad looked at Mum. They both looked at Luke.

"The biggest bucket we've got," Luke added, with a nod.

"We don't have any buckets anyway," Mum pointed out. "I've got this yoghurt pot. I could clean that out for you."

Luke's heart sank. A yoghurt pot? What good would that be? He could just imagine Ellie trying to stand in a yoghurt pot. He stomped off to school in a very, very bad mood, with an invisible Ellie beside him. Luke knew she was there because she was making such a fuss.

"What do you mean, you haven't got a bucket?" she moaned.

"I mean we don't have one," Luke said.

"Everybody has buckets," said Ellie.

"Well maybe they did a hundred years ago, but they don't now."

"You're useless," Ellie said. "I wish I hadn't bothered. I wish I'd never seen you in the bath. I wish I'd never said I'd go to your school. I wish ..."

"I wish you'd shut up!" shouted Luke, just as they passed the bus stop. Six people turned to stare at him.

"Who do you think you're telling to shut up?" demanded an old man at the front of the line.

Luke hurried on. "Be quiet, will you?" he hissed to Ellie. "You're just getting me into more and more trouble."

"Huh! All you do is think about yourself," snapped Ellie. "You think you're in trouble? I've been in trouble for almost a hundred years."

"Yeah? Well maybe you should have thought about that before you got on the *Titanic*," said Luke, even though he knew it was unkind.

"I didn't want to drown!" Ellie yelled back.

They both sank into a black silence after that. Luke wondered what he would do when they reached school. If he couldn't get enough water they wouldn't see Ellie and everyone would laugh at him again, especially Jack.

As he walked into class the other children turned to look at him. Luke knew why. They were expecting to see Ellie. Jack grinned broadly and went "Woooooooo!" under his breath and a few children giggled. Mrs Rubble eyed them over the top of her glasses.

"Time to see what you've done for your projects on the Victorians," she said. "First of all I would like you all to hold up your work so I can see it." Twenty-six hands went up with twenty-six projects. Mrs Rubble's eyes scanned the room.

"Luke," she said. "You don't seem to be holding any work in your hand. Have you done it?"

"Yes," said Luke.

"It must be invisible then," said Mrs Rubble. Luke almost laughed. That was the problem. His project – Ellie – *was* invisible!

"Well, Luke, I think you had better explain why you have nothing to show," Mrs Rubble said.

Luke took a deep breath. There was nothing for it now but to tell the truth. So he stood up and told Mrs Rubble and everyone about the bathroom and Ellie and the *Titanic*. Jack began to snigger. Grace began to laugh. Soon the whole class was chuckling away as if the whole thing was the best joke they had heard in ages. Of course, it would have helped if Ellie had actually spoken up for Luke, but she was still in the huff.

Luke felt himself getting crosser and crosser and hotter and hotter and redder and redder. He couldn't bear all that laughter banging away in his ears.

"A ghost that can only appear when she's wet?" said Mrs Rubble. "Oh Luke, I have heard

lots of mad excuses for not doing homework, but that is the maddest ever!"

"It's true!" Luke shouted, but the class just laughed even louder. "All I need is a bucket of water!"

"A bucket of water!" said Mrs Rubble, and she had to sit down she was laughing so hard. Tears were running down her cheeks.

That was it. Luke had had enough. He
stormed to the front of the class, grabbed the
goldfish bowl with both arms and threw all of
it at Ellie. It was a bit of a shame that Mrs
Rubble was sitting behind where Ellie was
standing because she got soaked too. But at
least the water worked. All of a sudden there
was Ellie, standing in a pool of water with a
fat goldfish in her hand.

"Oh my!" cried Mrs Rubble, and she fainted.

"Oh!" moaned Grace, and she fainted too.

Jack was completely silent. That was because he'd fainted ages before.

Chapter 8
Charlie's Grave

Ellie stood there, soaked to the skin, and completely visible. Luke looked at the class and their open mouths and their google eyes. He smiled, put some water in the bowl and held it out so Ellie could drop the goldfish in.

"This is Ellie," he told them. "She drowned when the *Titanic* sank. Now she is trying to find where Charlie Smith is buried because they were about to get married. Ellie can't rest in peace until she finds Charlie again."

The class just stared in silence at the thin ghost.

"It's all right," Luke said. "You can talk to her."

"Yes, say something!" said Ellie. "Stop looking at me like I'm a ... ghost." She giggled when she said that.

"Are ... you ... really ... dead?" asked Jack, who had woken from his faint.

"Are ... you ... really ... stupid?" Ellie answered back. "Of course I'm dead. Do you think I would look like this if I weren't?"

Jack said nothing. Mrs Rubble had also come round by this time so Luke began to explain about his project.

"I have been doing my work with Ellie here," he said. "She is going to tell you all what it was like to be on the *Titanic* when it sank."

And so that is what Ellie did, and she did it very well, because she had really been there. She brought every moment of the sinking to life for the class. When she got to the bit when she and Charlie lost their grip on each other and she drowned, almost everyone was in tears. Mrs Rubble did a lot of sniffing.

At the end some of the children clapped and Ellie gave them a little curtsey. Then Jack came up with a bright idea.

"Hey, why don't we split up after school and go to all the graveyards we can find and search for Charlie Smith's grave?" he said.

Luke was pleased and cross at the same time. It was a great idea, but Luke wished he had thought of it for himself.

"Jack's not as stupid as I thought," said Ellie, which made Luke even more cross.

After school the children went on a grave hunt and it was not long before Grace came back with some good news. She had found a grave with Charlie Smith's name on it, and the right date – 1915. Ellie had dried off by this time. Luke had to hunt round the graveyard until he found a watering can beside a tap. It was for watering plants on the graves but Luke had a better use for it. He gave Ellie a good sprinkling. They could see her again.

Ellie gazed at Charlie's grave for a long time. "At last," she sighed. "We can be together at last." She turned to Luke and the class. "Thank you," she said. "Thank you for everything. It's been a long wait."

Ellie hovered over the old grave for a minute and then very slowly, bit by bit, she

sank into the ground. Her feet vanished first, then her legs, then her body and at last her smiling face. Then she was gone. There was nothing but the peace and quiet of the old graveyard.

When Luke had a bath that night he covered himself in plenty of bubbles, just in case. But there was no sign of Ellie. He did get a surprise when he went into school on Monday morning, though.

Mrs Rubble was sitting behind her desk. There was a rather evil smile on her face.

"Luke," she began. "I think we have a problem. You didn't do your project last week."

"Yes I did!" said Luke. "Everyone saw! It was Ellie and the *Titanic*!"

"Exactly!" cried Mrs Rubble in triumph. "And the *Titanic* sank in 1912. That was nine

Pop!

years after Queen Victoria died, so it did NOT happen in Victorian times. You'll have to start all over again!"

Luke was gobsmacked. After everything he'd done. He'd brought a real ghost to school and it still wasn't enough for Mrs Rubble!

Mohammed put up his hand. "Mrs Rubble, Luke did do his project. Ellie was eighteen when she died and that means she was born five years BEFORE Queen Victoria died. Ellie was a Victorian."

"Yes!" cried the whole class. "Ellie was a Victorian. So there!"

"All right," muttered Mrs Rubble. "Don't get your knickers in a twist. OK, Luke's done his project."

Luke let out a sigh of relief. He wasn't very good at History. He wasn't much better at Maths either. In fact, he didn't even have a best subject. It was a good thing Mohammed was there to help him.

Luke winked at Mohammed and his friend beamed back a broad smile.

Our books are tested
for children and young people by
children and young people.

Thanks to everyone who consulted on
a manuscript for their time and effort in
helping us to make our books better
for our readers.